Work, Work, Work

WORK, WO

Story & Pictures by Daniel Quinn

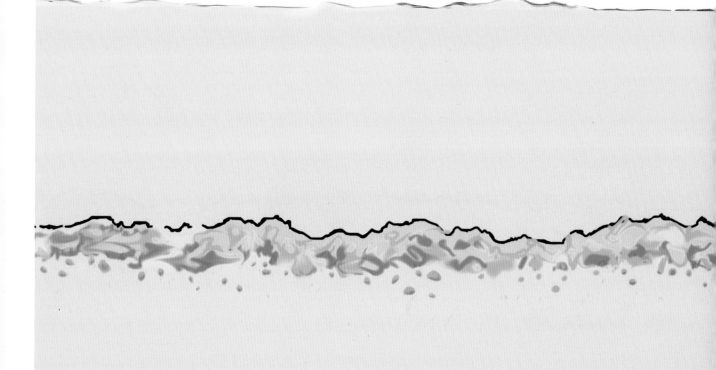

RK, WORK

STEERFORTH PRESS
Hanover, New Hampshire

For Daniel Fleischer, who rescued my mole.

zzzzz

DIG.
DIG.
DIG.

DIG,
DIG,
DIG.

BURROW,
BURROW,
BURROW.

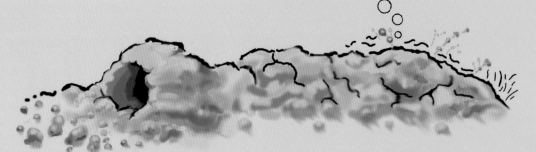

JUST DIG, DIG, DIG,
BURROW, BURROW,
BURROW.

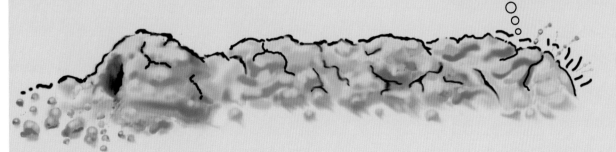

EVERY DAY
JUST LIKE THE
ONE BEFORE.

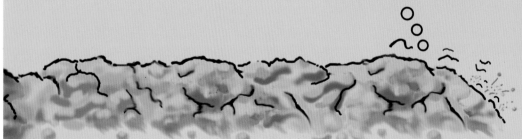

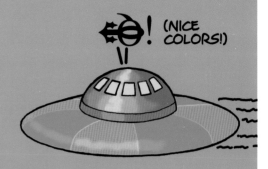

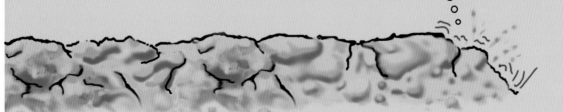

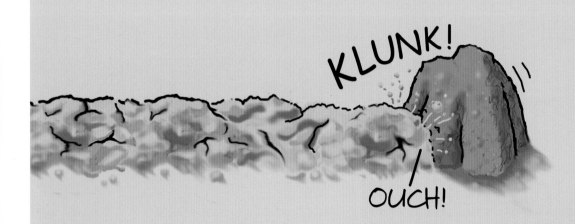

AND
SOMETIMES
YOU RUN
INTO A ROCK.

SOME DAYS YOU DON'T
EVEN RUN INTO A ROCK.

IS THE WORLD JUST
PASSING ME BY?

THAT'S WHAT I'D
LIKE TO KNOW.

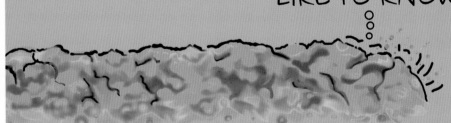

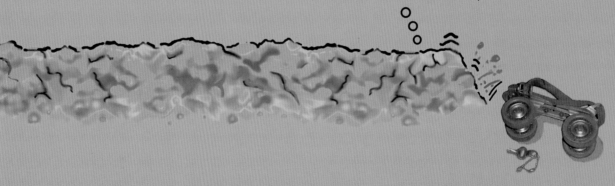

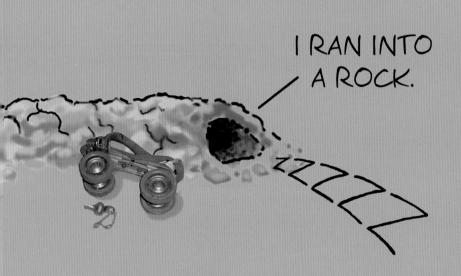